100 FACTS DOGS & PUPPIES

Camilla de la Bédoyère
Consultant: Steve Parker

SCHOLASTIC

ACKNOWLEDGEMENTS

The publishers would like to thank the following artists who have contributed to this book: Mark Davis (Mackerel), Peter Dennis (Linda Rogers Associates), John Dillow (Beehive Illustration), Mike Foster (Maltings Partnership), Richard Hook (Linden Artists), MagicGroup, Andrea Morandi, Julia Pewsey (Linden Artists), Steve Roberts, Eric Rowe (Linden Artists), Mike Saunders, Mike White (Temple Rogers).

Picture credits: All photographs courtesy of **Shutterstock** unless noted as follows: **Aardvark Animation/pictorialpress.com:** 46br (Wallace and Gromit); **gettyimages.com:** 37m (huskies in the snow); **N. Rotteveel:** 46tr (Greyfriars Bobby statue); **topfoto.co.uk:** 43bl (trench dog); **Warren Photographic:** 26bm (puppies playing), 27mr (puppy playing with toy), 28–29b (Staffordshire bull terriers).

Every effort has been made to acknowledge the source and copyright holder of each picture. The publishers apologize for any unintentional errors or omissions.

CONTENTS

OUR BEST FRIENDS

1

Dogs are special animals that have earned a place in our hearts and our homes. They have been close companions for people since the earliest times and they still work and play with us today. Dogs are clever creatures with strong, athletic bodies. They are alert and playful and they can move with great speed and agility.

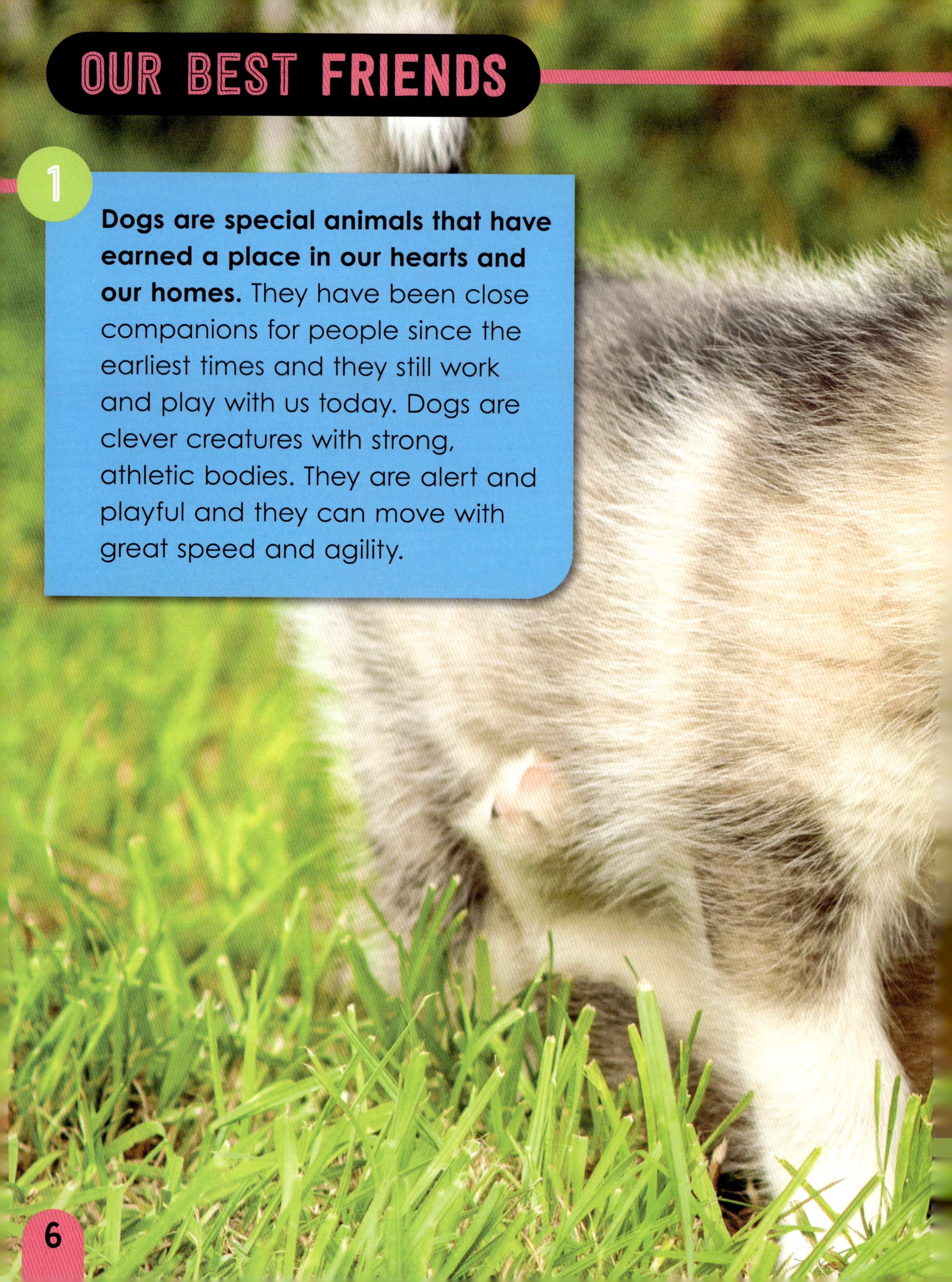

All dogs are mammals. They have warm blood, fur and they feed their babies with milk.

▶ From fearsome wolf to favourite pet, all members of the dog family are fascinating creatures. They have lots of energy, like these puppies, and are highly intelligent.

IN THE FAMILY

2 **There are wild dogs and domestic dogs, but they all belong to a family of animals called canids.** There are 36 different types (species) of canids, which includes wolves, foxes, coyotes and jackals, as well as the domestic dog. Canids are intelligent animals with long, lean bodies, slender legs and bushy tails.

▲ Jackals live in Africa, Asia and southern Europe. They will sometimes move into cities in the search of food and scraps.

3 **Domestic dogs are tame and live with people.** They are all one species of animal, which means that they can breed (mate) with one another. Different types of domestic dog are called breeds and there are around 350 recognized breeds, but new breeds are always being created.

◀ By mating two different types of domestic dog, it is possible to create an entirely new breed.

Canids are carnivores, which means they hunt and eat meat.

I DON'T BELIEVE IT!

One of the world's smallest dogs was a Yorkshire terrier. Even when fully grown this tiny pooch was still small enough to sit on your hand!

4 **Wild dogs are found almost all over the world.** Many species of wild dog are in danger of dying out because they are being hunted, or due to the places they live being taken over by people. Domestic dogs live almost everywhere that humans live.

▼▶ The tiny fennec fox and huge grey wolf may differ in size, but they are both members of the dog family and share many characteristics.

▼ Grey wolf

◀ Fennec fox

5 **The smallest wild dog is the fennec fox.** It is as small as a pet cat and lives in the desert lands of North Africa where it hunts lizards and bugs. The fennec fox has very large ears in relation to its body size, which allow it to pick up very quiet sounds, even over long distances.

6 **The largest wild dog is the grey wolf.** This magnificent creature can measure up to 1.5 metres in length, from its nose to its rump, and can weigh up to 60 kilograms. Some domestic dogs are even bigger. Great Danes are one of the tallest breeds and they can easily measure more than 2 metres in length.

CALL OF THE WILD

7 **African wild dogs live in huge packs that have more than 30 members.** They used to roam across the African plains hunting zebra, antelope and wildebeest. Sadly, there are not many packs of African wild dogs left now, as many have been caught in traps, shot by humans, or died from diseases spread by domestic dogs.

▶ African wild dogs have lost their homelands (habitat) to people or other animals and they are now in danger of extinction.

8 **The Arctic fox is pure white in winter to blend in with the snow.** Its fluffy winter coat is warm, and thick tufts of fur cover the fox's paws. During the summer the fox grows a thinner coat that is grey or brown.

9 **The red fox is a very common member of the dog family.** It is found all over Europe, Asia, North America and Australia. Like other foxes, these animals dig underground burrows where they can raise their cubs and stay warm. A fox's burrow is called an earth or a den.

▼ Red foxes are very adaptable and can live almost anywhere, and eat almost anything.

10

Most foxes will eat almost anything! Foxes that live in the countryside usually eat rabbits or young hares. They lie in wait in tall grass or bushes, and creep close to their prey – before suddenly leaping into action. They will also eat beetles, fruit, mice, berries, worms, frogs or food left around by humans.

▶ Coyotes live alone, in pairs, or in packs. Males may fight one another to protect their territories or hunting areas.

11

Coyotes are very fast runners and can reach speeds of 65 kilometres an hour when chasing their prey. These wolflike wild dogs live in North and Central America, and at night their howling can be heard across mountains and plains. Coyotes often live near to humans and have been known to attack family pets and even children.

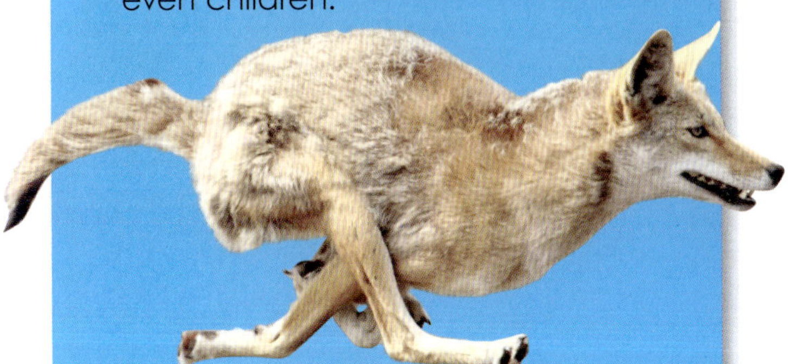

12

Wild dogs in Australia are called dingoes. It is thought that dingoes might have been domesticated at some point long ago, and have returned to living wild. They are now regarded as pests by many farmers, who build large dingo-proof fences to protect their sheep.

WOLVES

13 **Grey wolves are the largest wild members of the dog family.** However, there are not many grey wolves left in the wild because their habitats have been destroyed by humans. Wolves have also been hunted for centuries, partly because people are scared of them – even though it is very rare for a wolf to attack a human.

14 **Grey wolves live in family groups.** Each group is called a pack and usually contains between 8 and 12 wolves, although some packs may have up to 20 members. Each pack has a leader, called the alpha wolf. The alpha wolf is usually a female and she rules the group. The alpha female and her mate are the only wolves that have cubs.

▼ Grey wolves mate towards the end of the winter and litters of 2 to 10 pups are born 9 weeks later. Other females in the pack help to look after the pups.

15

Grey wolves work as a group to catch their prey. By hunting together, the wolves can chase, attack and kill animals that are much larger than themselves, such as bison and caribou. They also eat small animals including beavers, hares and rabbits. Wolves find their prey using their powerful senses of smell and hearing.

16

There are about 23 red wolves alive in the wild today. Red wolves are smaller than their grey cousins and they only live in North Carolina, USA. They mostly eat mice, rats and rabbits, but they will also eat berries and insects.

TELLING TALES

You can probably think of some stories or fairy tales where the spotlight is on a bad wolf.

Can you make up a story where the wolf is the hero instead?

Use words that describe the wolf's appearance and character.

Draw a picture to go with your story.

TAMING THE DOG

17 **Dogs were probably first tamed by humans around 12,000 years ago during the last ice age.** These first 'pet' dogs were most likely bred from wild wolves and dogs. They may have been used to hunt, or to scare off more dangerous wild animals, such as bears. Dogs were also used as protection on long journeys.

▲ The Spanish explorer Vasco de Nuñez Balboa took his dog Leoncico on all his expeditions and even paid him a wage.

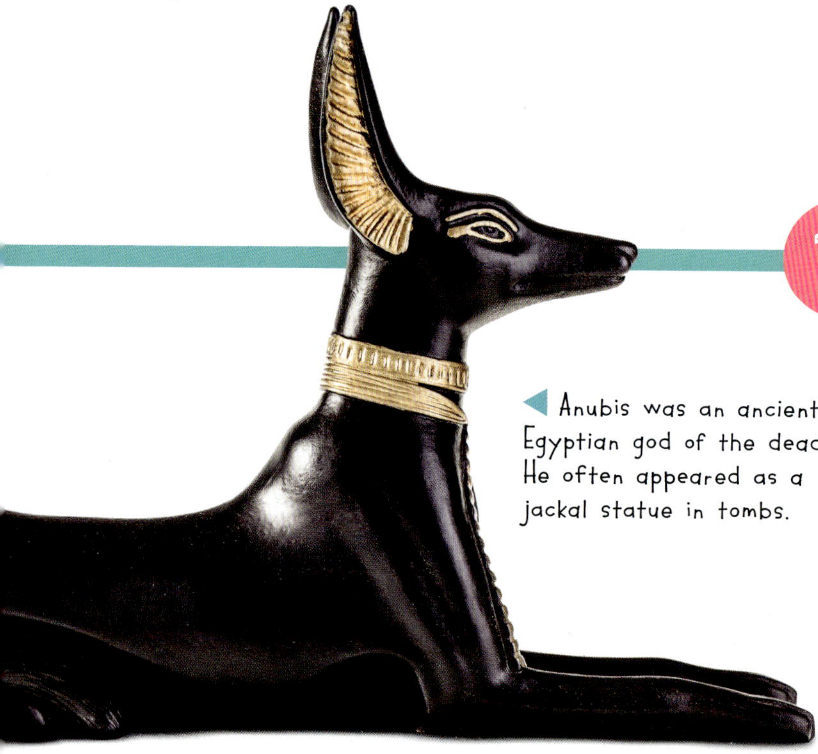

◀ Anubis was an ancient Egyptian god of the dead. He often appeared as a jackal statue in tombs.

18 **Ancient Egyptians had their dogs mummified so they could accompany them into the next life.** Dogs were prized as pets by Egyptians, but they also worked as guard dogs or hunters. Their proud owners gave them leather collars and names such as Brave One.

▶ Called a Chinese foo dog, this statue rests his paw on a ball that represents the Earth.

19 **Dogs have been treated like gods and used in worship.** Statues of lionlike dogs are often placed outside temples in the Far East, where they are believed to stand guard and protect the building from evil spirits.

20

Japanese ruler Tokugawa Tsunayoshi changed the law to protect dogs. He was so fond of his canine friends he decreed that any person who mistreated, or even ignored, a dog could be put to death. In one month alone, more than 300 people were executed as a result.

I DON'T BELIEVE IT!

Nine hundred years ago the king of Norway handed his throne to a dog! The royal pet ruled for three years and signed important papers with a paw print!

21

The Romans bred huge, vicious dogs, called Molossians, to fight in battles. These 'dogs of war' were similar to modern Rottweilers and, according to legend, Alexander the Great (a military leader of the ancient world) owned one beast that fought and killed an elephant and a lion. Romans also set up fights between dogs and slaves.

22

In England, dogs helped to protect travellers. Highwaymen used to hold up horse-drawn carriages and rob the people travelling in them. Dogs were trained to run alongside the carriages, and attack or frighten the highwaymen.

▼ Dalmatians were often used to protect the travellers in coaches because they are excellent guard dogs.

A DOG'S BODY

23 **The first doglike animal lived about 30 million years ago.** Around 300,000 years ago the first wolves appeared, and all of today's dogs descend from them. The way that animals change over time is known as evolution.

▼ Like all mammals, a dog's skeleton is made of bone – a tough but lightweight material. Muscles are attached to the skeleton by rubbery tendons.

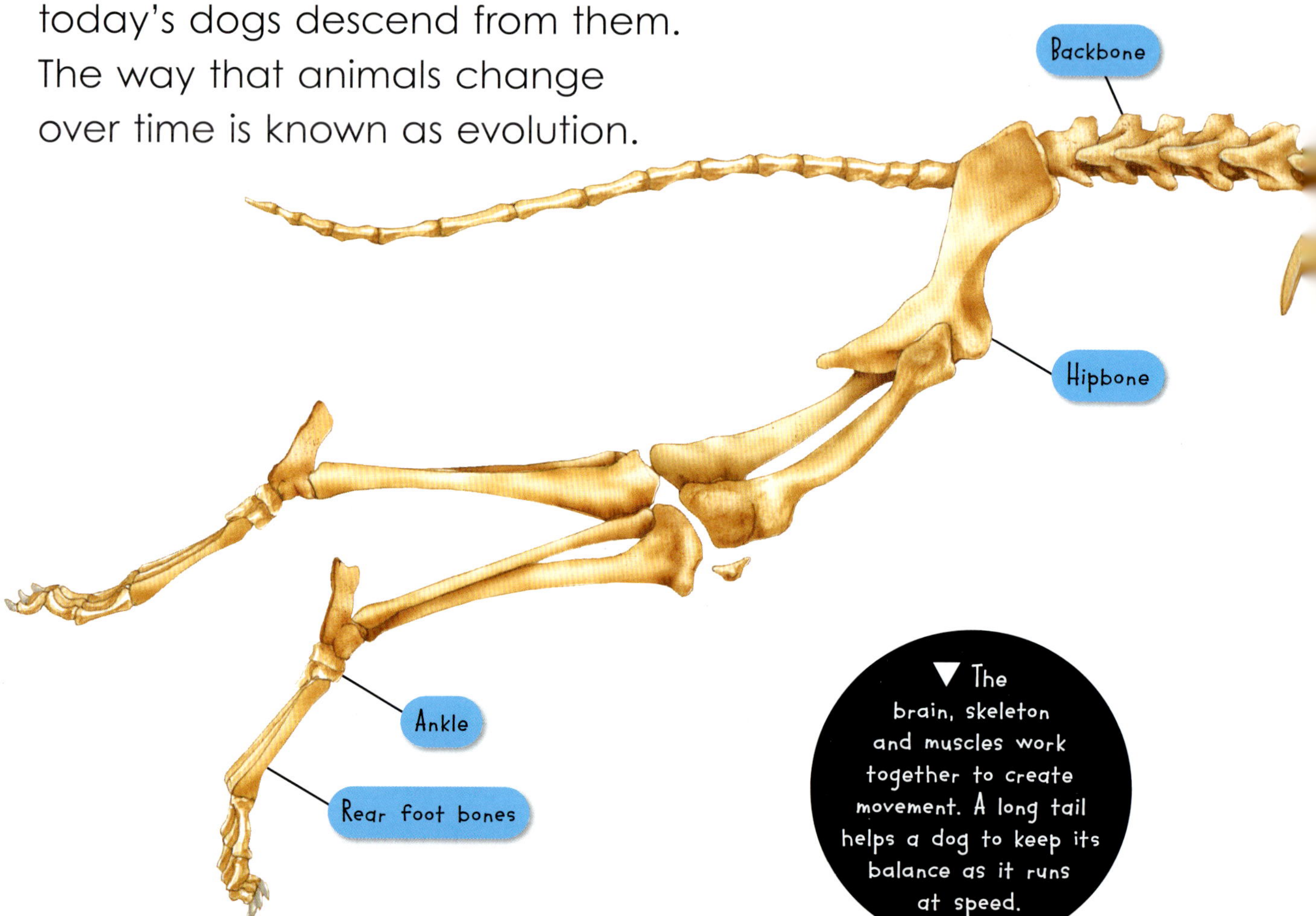

▼ The brain, skeleton and muscles work together to create movement. A long tail helps a dog to keep its balance as it runs at speed.

24 **All members of the dog family are similar in important ways.** Most canids have deep, muscle-packed chests, long bodies and strong, slender legs. Dogs are endurance runners. This means that they can keep running at a steady pace for a long time without tiring.

If we describe something as 'dog-eared' we mean it is shabby and worn out.

25

A dog's back paws have just four claws each, but its front paws have five claws. Domestic dogs, however, sometimes have extra claws on their back paws, called 'dew claws'. They are shorter, and are not used for walking.

▶ Dogs' claws, unlike cats' claws, are blunt and cannot be pulled back into the paw.

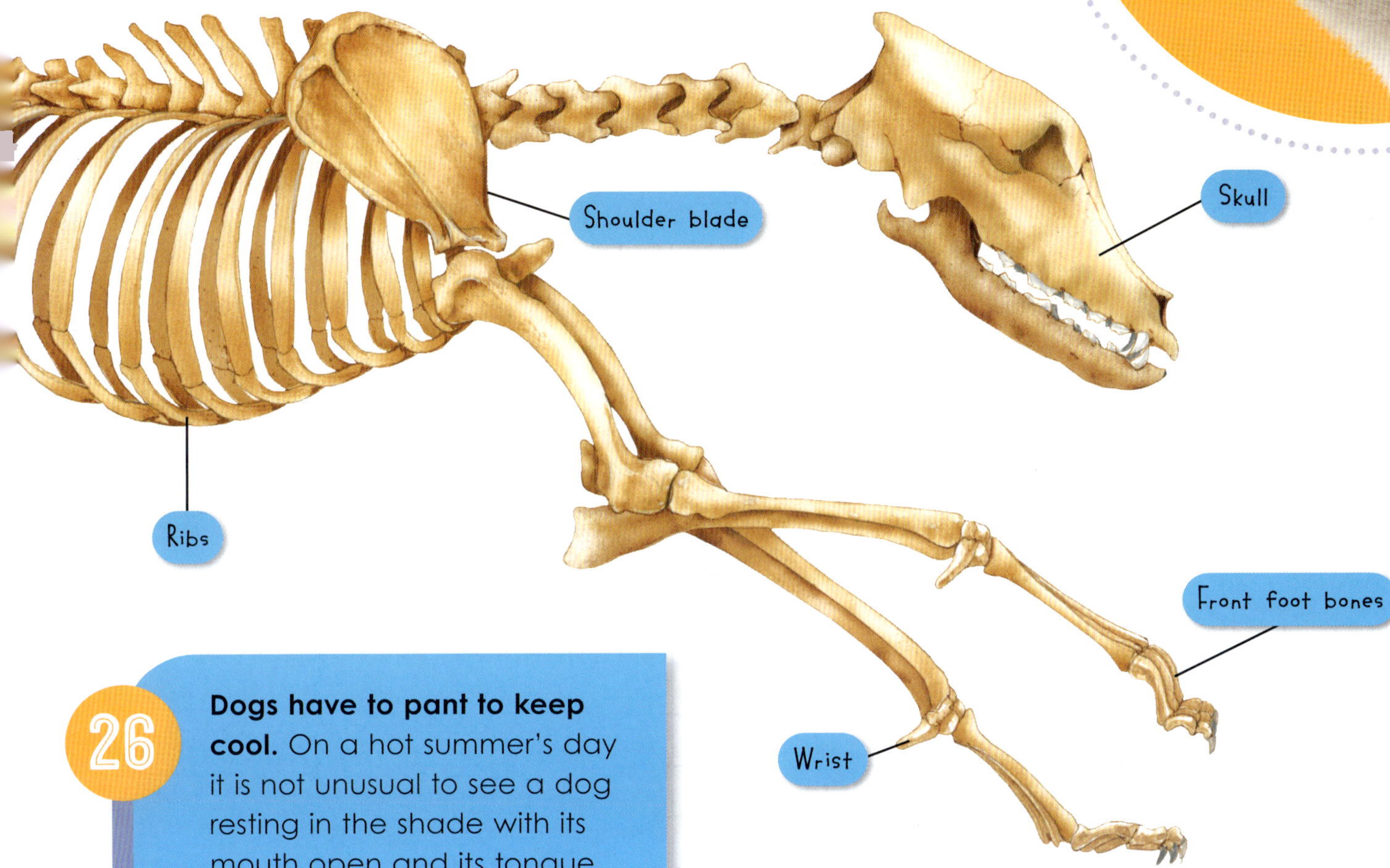

26

Dogs have to pant to keep cool. On a hot summer's day it is not unusual to see a dog resting in the shade with its mouth open and its tongue hanging out. This is a dog's unique way of cooling itself down. Unlike us, dogs cannot sweat when they get too hot. As the watery saliva on the dog's tongue evaporates (dries) the tongue cools. This lowers the dog's body temperature.

27

A dog's body is supported and protected by its skeleton, which is made up of many bones. The brain is protected by a hard, bony case called the skull. A dog's skull has to be unusually long to make room for its muzzle, which contains the nose and mouth.

SCRATCH AND SNIFF!

28 **Dogs have a much better sense of smell than humans.** They are particularly good at sniffing out certain scents such as sweat. In fact, it has been estimated that domestic dogs are one million times better at smelling sweat than us and they can even match a person to the smell of their sweat!

▶ Dogs such as this basset hound have around 220 million smell-sensing cells in their noses. Humans only have 20 million.

▼ Pointer dogs are popular hunting dogs. When they smell a game bird they stand still and 'point' with their bodies.

29 **Dogs can follow a trail using only their sense of smell.** Dogs such as bloodhounds have been used for centuries by police to find missing people and criminal suspects by tracking their scent. Bloodhounds have followed four-day old trails over distances of more than 120 kilometres.

Dogs can hear sounds that are too high for our ears to detect.

30

A strong sense of smell helps wild members of the dog family to survive. Wolves sniff the air to find out if other wolves are invading their territory. Wolf packs mark their territories with urine, and the smell contains a message telling other wolves to stay away. They also use their sense of smell to find a mate or their prey.

▼ The outer part of an ear is called the pinna. Many canids can move the pinna so it 'catches' a sound and directs it towards the eardrum, which sends the message to the brain.

31

Members of the dog family have eyes that help them follow the movement of other animals. This helps them chase down their prey. Some dogs, such as greyhounds, have very good eyesight but most types of dog can see less well than humans. Like cats, dogs are able to see some colours and have good vision in the evening and early morning when there is little natural light.

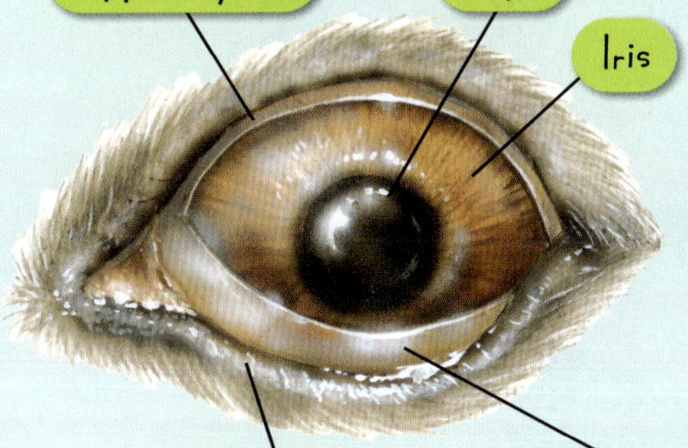

◀ Dogs have a membrane (skin) called the 'third eyelid' that protects their eyeballs. It sweeps across the eye to clear away dust and dirt.

32

Wolves' ears are large, upright and pointed, but modern domestic dogs have ears in a huge variety of shapes and sizes. Wild dogs can move their ears in the direction of a sound, to help the animal hear it better. Some dog breeds have long, drooping ears that cannot be so easily moved.

BODY LANGUAGE

33 **Dogs are social animals.** This means that they like to live with other animals, or humans. In the wild, a group of dogs usually has a leader – the 'top dog'. The 'top dog' decides what the group will do, and the 'underdogs' follow his, or her, lead. Pet dogs treat their owners as if they are the 'top dogs' of the pack, and that's why they can be trained to be obedient.

I DON'T BELIEVE IT!

In 1960 two Russian dogs – Strelka and Belka – became famous as the first dogs to go into space and return safely to Earth. The courageous canines travelled around the planet 18 times before landing.

34 **Dogs show how they are feeling using their mouths, ears and tails.** Frightened dogs will put their tails between their legs. They flatten their ears against their heads and may even roll over onto their backs. This is a dog's way of showing that it does not want to fight.

◀ A dog's body language can show how it is feeling. This dog is scared and, by making its body seem small, it is asking other dogs – or humans – to leave it alone.

Labradors and Alsatians have better eyesight than most other breeds of dog.

35

Growling, barking and howling are a dog's way of sending messages to other animals. Wolves howl and dogs growl to warn other animals to stay away. Barking is a dog's way of telling other members of its pack that something strange is happening, and to be alert and on guard.

▶ Wolves howl rather than bark and some pet dogs communicate this way too. Howling can be heard over great distances.

36

Young puppies do not wag their tails. Dogs usually start tail-wagging when they are four to six weeks old, normally when they are feeding on their mother's milk. Older dogs often wag their tails when they are excited about seeing another friendly dog or a person that they know.

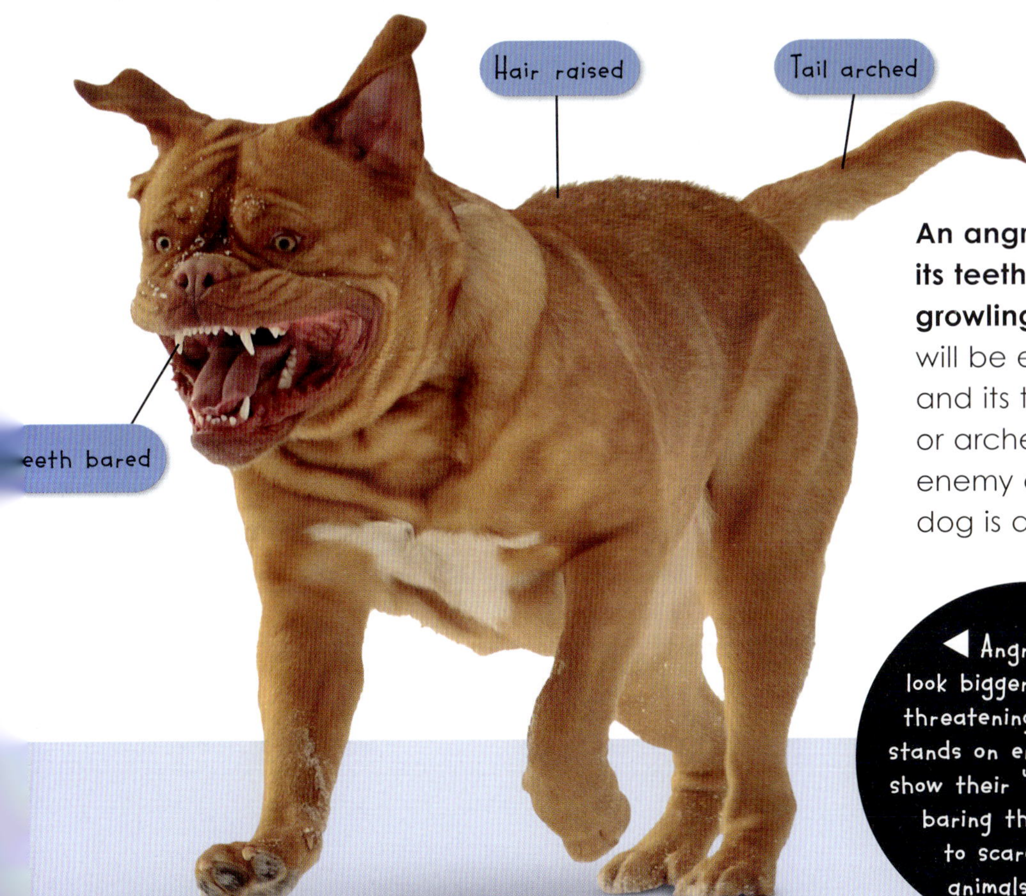

37

An angry, aggressive dog will bare its teeth in a menacing way, while growling. If it can prick its ears they will be erect and pointing forward and its tail will be held out straight or arched up behind. This shows the enemy animal or person that the dog is alert and ready for action.

◀ Angry dogs look bigger and more threatening. Their fur stands on end and they show their 'weapons' by baring their teeth to scare other animals away.

A DOG'S DINNER

38 **All canids are hunters.** Dogs, both wild and domestic, have a natural instinct to look for creatures to chase, kill and eat. Animals that hunt other animals are called 'predators' and the animals they hunt are called 'prey'. Both dogs and cats are predators, but dogs (unlike cats) rarely live on a diet of meat alone and may eat fruit and insects too.

39 **Many dogs enjoy chewing beef bones and this helps to keep their teeth clean and their gums healthy.** Bones can break and splinter, however, so pet dogs should only be allowed to chew bones for a short while. It is better if they chew on special toys that are designed to massage their gums. These can be made of meat, biscuit, rubber, nylon or braid.

40 **Pet dogs do not need to hunt for their food.** Dog owners give their pets regular meals – usually cooked meat and biscuits with added vitamins and minerals. Dogs are often given small treats to reward them for good behaviour, but these should only be given as part of their training, as they are not part of a healthy diet.

▼ Pet dogs eat a range of food, not just meat. Biscuits and dental chews provide extra vitamins and help keep a dog's teeth clean. Dogs need plenty of fresh water every day.

It is not unusual for domestic or wild dogs to chew grass.

41

Chocolate is dangerous to dogs. Although many dogs like the taste of chocolate they shouldn't be allowed to eat it, because even a tiny amount is enough to poison a small dog. Dog treats will normally contain very little chocolate, or none at all.

42

Dogs can suffer from gum disease and bad breath – just like people! Dog owners can brush their pets' teeth to help keep them clean and avoid decay. You shouldn't use human toothpaste on a dog's teeth as it contains fluoride, which can poison a dog, but you can buy special toothpaste for dogs, which you can get from vets. You should check a dog's mouth regularly, looking for bad and broken teeth or swollen gums and lips.

DINER OR DINNER?

These animals are either predators, or prey. Find the predators and the prey:

- **A** Wolf
- **B** Rabbit
- **C** Polar Bear
- **D** Cheetah
- **E** Rhinoceros
- **F** Zebra

Answers: Predator: a c d Prey: b e f

STARTING A FAMILY

43 **Female dogs are usually pregnant for between 60 and 70 days.** During this time the pups grow slowly inside her. A pregnant female needs to be treated with care. She will tire more easily and needs short exercise periods. Pregnant dogs need more food towards the end of their pregnancy.

▲ This Labrador puppy is a newborn, and cannot survive without its mother's care. She feeds it with milk and keeps it warm, clean and safe.

44 **In the wild, most dogs have their puppies (cubs) in a safe place called a den, or an earth.** The den may be a hole in the ground, or a cave. It needs to be dry, dark and hidden so that the youngsters are protected from other animals. Domestic dogs will also make 'nests' where they feel safe enough to give birth. The ideal place is in a quiet corner where they will not be disturbed.

▶ When a puppy is 2 weeks old its eyes and ears should be working, so it will begin to take more interest in its surroundings, although it cannot yet stand properly or walk.

▶ At 3 weeks old a puppy can move clumsily and snuggles up to its littermates to sleep. Like human babies, puppies need plenty of rest.

45 **When female dogs are ready to give birth they often stop eating.** Most will also become very restless for a few hours before birthing begins. They need to be kept away from other animals and allowed to settle quietly into their nest. When they begin to give birth they are said to be 'whelping'.

Puppies are very curious animals and they will sniff, eat and chew almost anything.

47 **A mother dog usually gives birth to a group, or litter, of between 3 and 8 pups, and looking after them is hard work.** All dogs are mammals – this means that their babies grow inside them, and they feed on their mother's milk when they are young. As soon as the puppies are born their mother licks them clean. At this age, puppies cannot eat solid food – they can only suck milk from their mother.

46 **Puppies are born deaf and blind and they rely on their mother to look after them.** During its first weeks of life a puppy spends most of its time asleep while its body grows and develops. After 10 to 14 days a puppy's eyes begin to open and after 14 days most puppies can sit up. They can't stand for another week, and a few days after that a puppy begins to walk.

▶ When a puppy reaches 5 weeks of age its mother begins to push it away when it tries to feed from her. At 6 weeks of age it will begin to eat solid food.

◀ Playful, curious and noisy – an 8-week-old puppy has its own personality. Soon it will leave its mother to meet a new family.

PUPPY LOVE

48 **Puppies should stay with their mothers until they are about 10 weeks old.** From this time they can be given to a new family. Looking after a puppy is a lot of work. They need four meals a day and lots of affection.

49 **Puppies love to play.** Young puppies play with their brothers and sisters, but as they grow older they play with people, too. When they play, puppies are practising skills they might need later in life – such as hunting, chasing and fetching.

I DON'T BELIEVE IT!

When pedigree dogs mate there is an increased chance that their puppies will have problems such as deafness. Over 80 breeds may be at risk of deafness.

▼ Young puppies play-fight with their brothers and sisters. Play-fighting may look aggressive, but it is just a dog's way of asserting its dominance and personality.

50

Puppies and adult dogs can get bored and restless if they do not get enough exercise. All dogs – especially young ones – need to spend plenty of time outdoors where they can explore using all their senses. Dogs love to follow the trail of a new smell and enjoy sniffing the ground and plants. Some dogs are natural 'diggers' and enjoy scratching at the ground, particularly on flowerbeds and lawns!

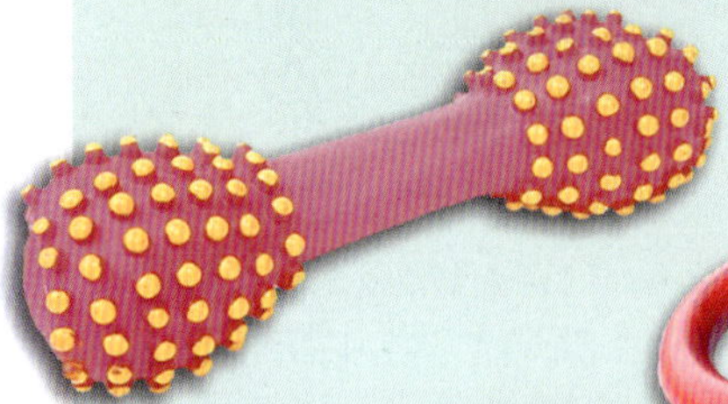

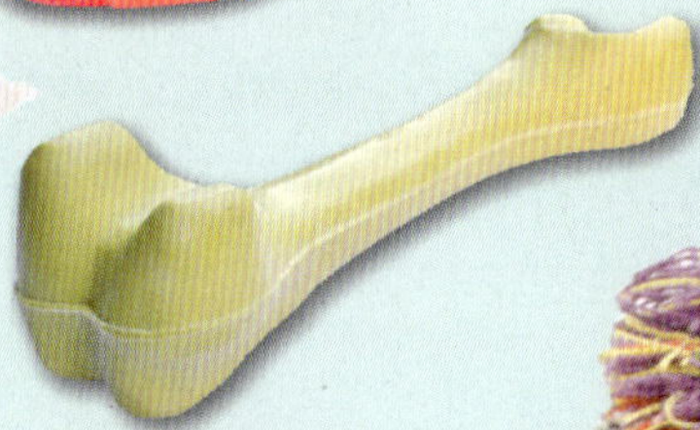

▶ Puppies love chewing toys, especially ones that squeak! Never give a dog a toy with small parts, as they could choke on them.

▲ Puppies must learn that they should play only with their own toys.

51

Toys are a great way to keep a puppy happy. Most dogs love to play with toys that they can chase and catch, such as balls and Frisbees. You can teach a dog to bring its toy back to you by rewarding it with a small treat or by praising it every time it fetches. When they are at home, puppies can turn almost anything into a toy and they love chewing on shoes and furniture.

DOGS ARE FOR LIFE

52 **Deciding to buy a dog is an important decision.** Caring for an animal is a big responsibility – it takes work and can be expensive. Before getting a dog you should find out how much care it will need by talking to other dog owners and vets, and by reading books and looking at websites.

53 **It can be best to buy a puppy rather than an adult dog, as you can make sure it has the best training and care from a young age.** It's a good idea to buy a puppy from a breeder, or a person recommended to you by a vet, because it is essential that the puppy has been well looked after in its first weeks of life.

54 **Dogs are sometimes abandoned by owners who don't want them anymore.** Occasionally, people realize, after getting a dog, that they are unable to look after their pet. Responsible owners will find a better home for their animal, but it is not unusual for dogs to be turned out into the street. Dogs that are abandoned are known as strays.

In 1987 a Great Dane gave birth to a massive litter of 23 puppies.

55

Dogs usually live for between 10 and 15 years, depending on their breed. They need to visit the vet for vaccinations, which will help protect them from disease, and to be treated for any injuries or illnesses they get during their active and busy lives. Good owners will check their dog regularly for any scratches, cuts or other signs of illness.

▶ Vets give dogs and puppies vaccinations to help protect them from a range of diseases such as distemper and kennel cough.

▼ Which of these Staffordshire bull terrier puppies would you choose? It is important to check a puppy for signs of good health, alertness and a pleasing personality. Try to visit a litter of puppies several times before making a choice.

56

Dogs need time, patience and attention. They need to be stroked, fed, walked and played with every single day. Young dogs should not be left alone all day as they can become lonely and difficult to train.

HOW MANY PUPS?

1. Three bitches (female dogs) have puppies. One of them has six puppies, while the other two have four puppies each. How many puppies are born altogether?
2. Daisy is a Dalmatian dog. She has five puppies every year for three years. How many puppies has she had altogether?

Answers: 1. 14 2. 15

CARING FOR A DOG

57 **A new puppy settles quickly into a home where preparations have been made for its arrival.** At first, it should be kept in one room or in a pen. It needs a bed. This can be a cardboard box to begin with, lined with old towels or pullovers to keep it warm.

58

Exercising a puppy on a lead helps it learn how to obey you. It is important that puppies and dogs learn to behave well and obey your commands, especially when they are outdoors with other animals and people. There are four basic commands – Sit, Stay, Come and Lie down. Once your dog has mastered these, you may want to try him or her out on a few more complicated instructions.

◀ When a dog follows a command correctly it is important to praise him or her. This Dalmatian is waiting patiently for his reward.

59

Dogs and puppies need to be kept safe when they are playing. They should not be allowed on the streets without a collar or a lead, in case they run into the road or scare people. If a dog lives in the countryside it must be kept away from farmers' animals. Responsible owners always clear up their pets' droppings.

▲ Cardboard boxes make good dens for a new puppy, but baskets are more suitable for older dogs.

Dogs love to roll in sand and dust. This soothes their skin and keeps their fur soft and clean.

60 **Dogs need to be groomed every day, especially long-haired breeds.** Brushing a dog's fur helps remove dead hairs and dirt, and keeps its coat glossy. Dogs also need baths sometimes to give them a deep-clean and keep them smelling sweet.

◀ Puppies should wear collars from an early age to get used to them. They can begin training to walk on a lead from the age of 12 to 15 weeks.

◀ Dog food contains vitamins and minerals that are an important part of a dog's daily diet. This complete food can be moist or dry.

61 **All dog equipment, such as feed bowls and toys, should be kept clean and germ-free.** Puppies need to have regular meals and it is possible to buy specially prepared dog food for them. Breeders usually give new dog owners a diet sheet that tells them which types of food are best for their pet.

▼ Regular grooming using a brush or a comb helps to keep a dog's coat clean and healthy.

62 **A puppy has to be house-trained.** This means that it needs to learn to go to the toilet outside the house. A very young puppy cannot control when it passes its waste. Whenever a young puppy wants to relieve itself place it on newspaper or a puppy pad and reward it when it finishes. Most puppies are house-trained by the time they are six months old.

PLAY THE GAME!

This is a game for a group, played just like musical bumps.

When the music stops, the leader must shout a command ('Sit', 'Stay', 'Come' or 'Lie down'). Everyone must follow the command correctly – the last person to do the correct action is out. The last person still playing is the winner.

DOG BREEDS

63 **There are many types (breeds) of domestic dog.** Dog breeds are divided into groups, according to their type. There are seven groups – working dogs, terriers, toy, herders, hounds, sporting dogs and utility (other). Some dogs are suited to family life and make good pets, but others thrive on a farm or enjoy a working life.

◀ Like German shepherds, mastiffs, boxers, dobermans and Dalmatians, Rottweilers are strong working dogs.

64 **Afghans are famous for their long, shaggy coats.** These tall and leggy dogs are an ancient breed that originally came from Afghanistan. Harsh winters meant that dogs from this area needed to have thick, warm coats. Afghans were once trained to hunt wolves, leopards and jackals, but now they make popular family pets.

▼ Afghans are hounds. This word is used to describe dogs that have been used to hunt wild animals in the past.

65 **The Rottweiler is an intelligent breed of working dog.** Originally from Germany, they are strong and powerful. The temperament of the Rottweiler can be unpredictable and they have been known to attack people, but with good training and control they can make excellent guard dogs.

A bloodhound's sense of smell is hundreds of times better than a human's.

66

The Chihuahua is the smallest breed of dog. In fact, they are not just small, they are tiny, reaching to between 16 and 20 centimetres in height! These dainty toy dogs need little exercise and they must be kept out of the cold.

▶ Chihuahuas are known as toy, or companion dogs. They are famous for their lively intelligence.

67

Herding dogs have been bred for their great intelligence and energy. They often work on farms, where they help the shepherds control the sheep, but many herding dogs are also used to do police work or are kept as family pets.

◀ Golden retrievers rarely work as sporting dogs today. They are popular family pets as they love being with children and are easy to train.

68

Sporting dogs are also known as gundogs. These animals were first bred to work with humans and flush out birds, hares and other animals to be shot. The dog then collected, or 'retrieved', the dead animal and brought it back to the hunter.

◀ Terriers can be quite snappy in nature and some bark a lot. Although some breeds love children, not all types suit a young family.

69

Terriers were bred to run underground and chase other animals out of their holes. Jack Russell terriers were named after the parson who first bred them. They were trained to run with the hounds during foxhunts, and chase the foxes out of their hiding places so the hounds could catch them.

PEDIGREES AND MONGRELS

70 **A dog whose ancestors – parents, grandparents and great grandparents – were all the same breed is called a pedigree, or purebred.** Pedigree dogs are usually very expensive to buy, but one advantage is that their owners know how large they will grow, and what their personalities will be like.

71 **Bulldogs might look fierce, but they are actually sweet-natured and make good pets for children.** Unfortunately they tire very easily and cannot walk long distances before needing a rest. They also get uncomfortable in hot weather and tend to breathe quite noisily. Bulldogs were originally bred to tackle bulls by grabbing their noses with their front teeth!

▲ Bulldogs have huge skulls and folds of loose skin, especially around their heads, necks and shoulders. They walk with a peculiar 'rolling' motion on their short, sturdy legs.

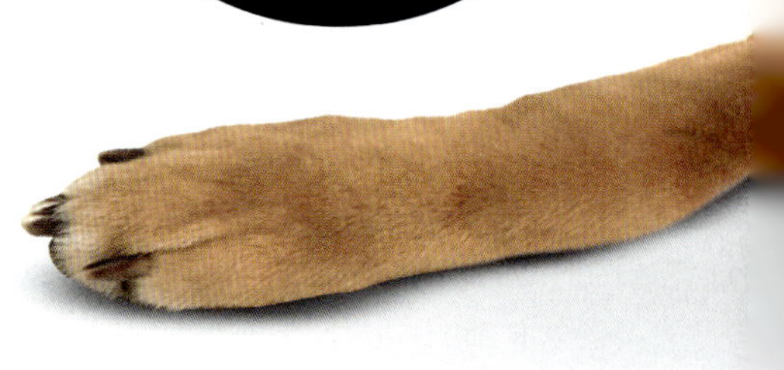

▶ Thousands of greyhounds are retired from racing every year and have to find new homes. Many become family pets.

72 **Greyhounds lived over 4000 years ago in ancient Egypt, and pictures of them were drawn on the walls of the pyramids.** These slender and athletic pedigrees are famous for their love of running and they are often bred and trained to take part in races. They have gentle natures and enjoy being with children.

Many dogs enjoy watching television programmes and movies.

73 **Dogs that are not pedigree or purebred are called mongrels.** Usually the breed of their parents is not known and they may be a mixture of lots of different breeds. Mongrels are often healthier than pedigree dogs. If a dog of one breed mates with a dog of another breed, the puppies are called cross-breeds.

▶ Mongrels can make great pets, but without knowing about their background it is difficult to know how their personalities will develop.

74 **Bloodhounds are famous for their droopy ears.** It is thought that they were first brought to Britain in 1066 by William the Conqueror. Bloodhounds have a fantastic sense of smell, and are often used as tracker dogs.

WHAT'S MY BREED?

Rearrange the letters to find the names of dog breeds:

1. **Gup**
2. **Gorci**
3. **Rexbo**
4. **Doolpe**
5. **Tearg aned**

Answers:
1. Pug 2. Corgi 3. Boxer 4. Poodle 5. Great Dane

SNOW DOGS

75 **For hundreds of years St Bernard rescue dogs searched through the Alps for people who needed their help.** Stranded by bad weather and avalanches, many climbers and walkers owed their lives to these noble dogs who braved the mountains to save them.

▶ There are several dog breeds that suit a cold climate. Once working dogs, Samoyeds are now popular as pets.

76 **Some breeds of dog have lived in the cold lands of the north for hundreds of years.** In these regions the winters are severe and thick snow makes it difficult for people to travel. By using a sledge, pulled by a team of dogs, it is easier to cover long distances and transport goods and food.

▶ Pyrenean mountain dogs are a giant breed and can weigh up to 65 kilograms!

◀ All St Bernard rescue dogs are now retired from work. Rescues in difficult conditions are now carried out by helicopter patrols with heat-seeking equipment.

Huskies make great 'hot-water bottles' for kids who live near the North Pole!

77

Huskies are one of the world's best known breeds of snow dogs. They can cope with cold weather because they have thick fur and can survive on much less food than other dogs of their size. Huskies have changed very little through breeding and are still very similar to their ancestor, the wolf – they howl, rather than bark, and they live in packs. Although huskies will pull sledges, they are difficult to train in any other way.

▲ A team of huskies can pull a sledge up to 130 kilometres in one day. Some huskies are specially bred to take part in speed sledge racing while others are bred to travel long distances.

78

Alaskan malamutes, Eskimo dogs and Samoyeds are all breeds of snow dog. Alaskan malamutes are similar to huskies but they are more affectionate. Eskimo dogs are now one of the rarest breeds, but they have worked alongside the Inuit people of the Arctic for thousands of years. Samoyeds are pale-coloured, good-natured dogs that are now most often kept as family pets.

UNUSUAL BREEDS

79 **There are many strange breeds of dog.** Some of these unusual breeds came about because they suit the places where they live, but others have been especially bred to exaggerate their most peculiar characteristics.

▲ The fluffy chow-chow belongs to one of the world's oldest dog breeds. They were first bred as herding dogs in Mongolia. Chow-chows have blue-black tongues.

80 **The Chinese crested dog is one of the most unusual-looking pets you will ever see.** This breed is small and almost completely hairless, except for sprouts of hair on its head, feet and tail. Chinese crested dogs make great pets but they must be covered in sunscreen on hot days and have to wear a coat on cold days.

◀ Chinese crested dogs are about 30 centimetres tall. They make popular pets as they are intelligent and do not need much exercise.

I DON'T BELIEVE IT!

The hair of Hungarian puli dogs grows to form thick cords that reach to the ground. Their fur needs constant combing to prevent it from forming a frizzy, knotted clump!

81

The wrinkliest dog is the Shar Pei. It has folds of skin around its head and face, a frowning expression and a bristly coat. Shar Peis were bred in China to herd sheep and hunt boar but they are now kept as pets. Shar Peis almost became extinct in their native China and were once considered the rarest dog breed in the world. The line was continued by breeders in Hong Kong and they have become more popular in recent years.

▼ Shar Peis are born with wrinkles all over their skin. As they get older, many of these wrinkles disappear, except for those around the face, neck and withers (shoulder area).

◀ Poodles need to have their thick, curly hair shampooed and clipped regularly.

82

Poodles come in all shapes, sizes and haircuts! It is thought that poodles could be one of the oldest dog breeds in the world, and their pictures appear on ancient Greek and Roman coins. There are three main types of poodle: standard, miniature and toy. Poodles do not moult (shed their hair), making them a good choice of dog for people with allergies and asthma.

83

The dog with the strangest name is the Xoloitzcuintle. Known as Xolos for short, these dogs are completely hairless. By the 1950s it was thought that this breed was so rare that it was going to die out, but since then it has become much more popular as a family pet.

CLEVER CLOGS

84 **Dogs are smart enough to learn new tricks.** They can learn how to roll over, beg and even shake hands. Dog owners can enter their dogs into competitions, where they are judged for their appearance or for their obedience skills. More than 20,000 dogs compete every year at the world's most famous dog show – Crufts.

85

Dogs can predict earthquakes and thunderstorms. When they know that a big natural event is going to happen, dogs may become alarmed, start panting and rush madly about the house or garden. They may get very distressed and begin to whimper and shake. It is possible that dogs are sensitive to tiny changes in air pressure before thunderstorms, or can hear an earthquake's first rumbles before humans can.

◀ Dogs that attend obedience trials perform tricks such as jumping over obstacles, coming when called and finding items touched by their owner.

A wolf can smell a deer 2 kilometres away.

I DON'T BELIEVE IT!

Dogs cannot see green, orange or red. Guide dogs learn to watch traffic lights and 'read' them by their brightness and position rather than by colour.

▲ Border collies crouch down and fix their gaze on the sheep. They herd the sheep without needing to bark or nip.

86

The world's cleverest dogs are Border collies, poodles and German shepherds. These breeds of dog are often chosen to work with humans because they can learn new commands very quickly and are usually very obedient. Border collies are often used as sheepdogs. They are able to follow instructions to help herd an entire flock of sheep into a pen.

◀ Grey fox cubs start to climb trees when they are only four weeks old.

87

Grey foxes can climb trees. You might usually expect to see cats in trees, but the grey tree fox, which lives in southern USA and Mexico, often makes its den in a hollow tree. It will climb trees to find its food – insects, birds and fruit – or to escape from danger. Grey foxes live in pairs rather than in a pack.

DOING GOOD WORK

88 **Some dogs have important jobs to do.** Dogs are easily trained, so they make excellent companions for people and many work in hospitals. It is thought that patients who have contact with animals recover faster than patients who do not.

89 **Service dogs are trained to help people.** During World War I dogs were trained to help blind soldiers who'd been wounded in battle. Since then, hundreds of thousands of dogs around the world have learned how to help people who can't see. Their work means that blind people have more freedom to get out and enjoy life.

▲ A building has been reduced to rubble, but this specially trained dog can use its great senses of smell and hearing to find any survivors.

◀ Guide dogs allow people who have little or no eyesight to be more independent.

I DON'T BELIEVE IT!

Service dogs can be trained to open doors, turn on switches and even help their owners take off their shoes and socks.

90

Dogs can be used to find dangerous chemicals, including bombs. Labrador retrievers and German shepherds are often used for this sort of work because of their extraordinary sense of smell. In the USA dogs are trained to sniff out more than 19,000 different combinations of exploding chemicals that can be used to make bombs. They can also detect drugs that are being smuggled in planes, cars, trucks and boats.

▼ Dogs that work with the police are trained to frighten and capture criminals as well as controlling crowds, or finding lost people. German shepherd dogs are popular because they are strong, intelligent and have an excellent sense of smell.

▼ 'Trench dogs' were popular with soldiers because they provided companionship and killed rats.

91

Dogs were used to carry messages during World War I. Many human messengers were killed so dogs were trained to do this task instead. Stray dogs were trained and sent to the front. Messages or food were put in tin cylinders and the dogs carried them between soldiers. The dogs probably saved many lives, but 7500 of them were killed in action.

92 **Cerberus was a terrifying many-headed dog that guarded the entrance to Hades, the Underworld in Greek mythology.** Cerberus allowed new spirits to enter the land of the dead, and prevented any spirits from leaving. Only a few ever managed to sneak past the creature. One story tells of a man named Orpheus, who lulled Cerberus to sleep by playing a lyre.

▲ Fierce Cerberus was no match for a Greek hero who lulled him to sleep with sweet music.

93 ***The Hound of the Baskervilles* is a story of demonic dogs and terrifying curses.** According to legend, every member of the Baskerville family would die after being attacked by a giant dog. In the story, ace detective Sherlock Holmes investigates and puts the curse to rest.

▶ Sir Arthur Conan Doyle wrote *The Hound of the Baskervilles* in 1902, basing it on ancient myths of evil dogs.

Enid Blyton, the famous children's writer, kept a fox terrier.

94

According to ancient Welsh legends, a wolfhound named Gelert saved the life of a prince's baby son. Gelert was protecting the baby when a wolf entered the nursery. Gelert fought the wild beast and killed it, but when the prince returned home he saw an empty cot and believed that Gelert had killed his child. He ran a sword through Gelert's heart, before finding his baby safe and well, and the body of the dead wolf.

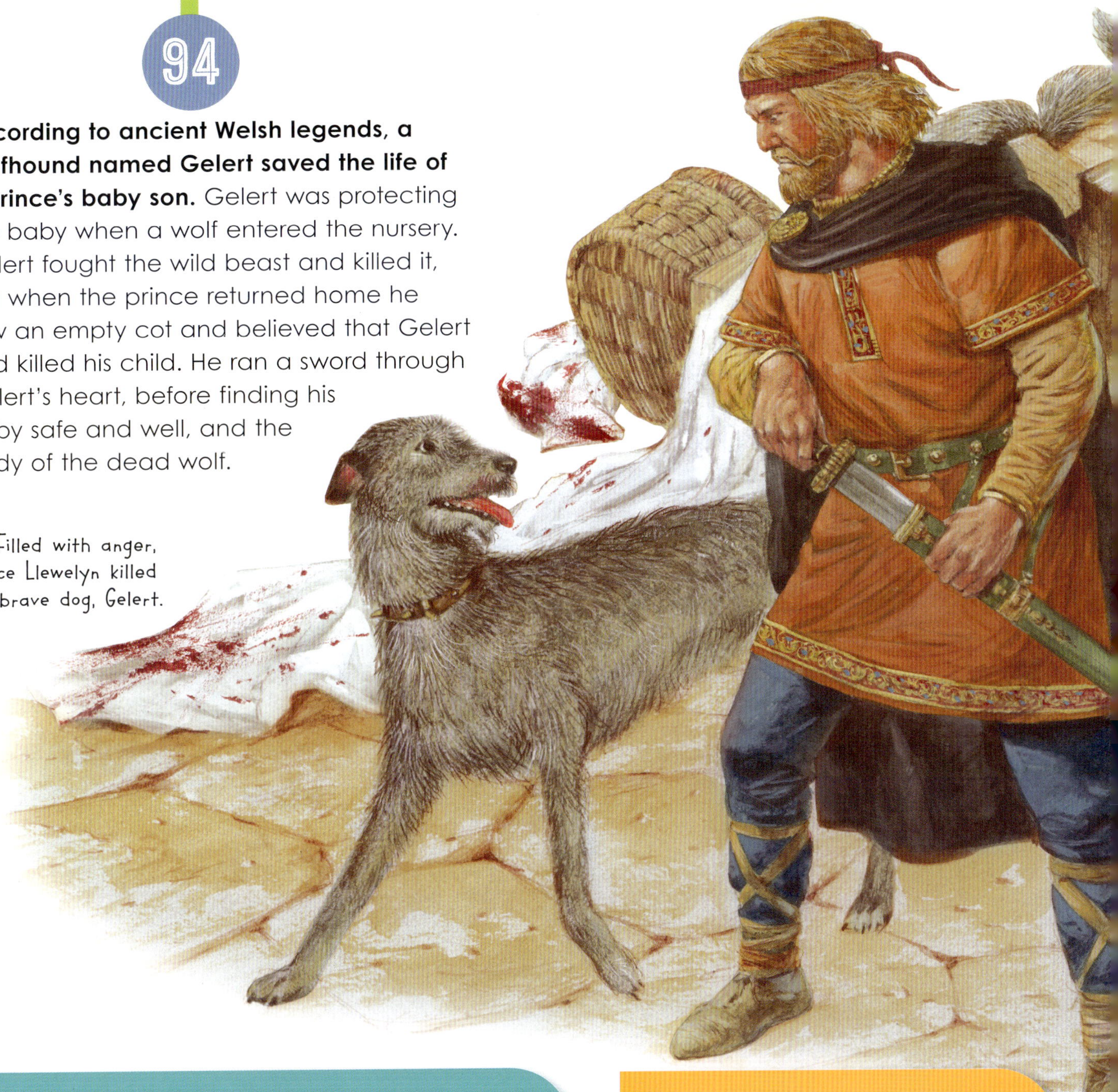

▶ Filled with anger, Prince Llewelyn killed his brave dog, Gelert.

95

Native Americans have lived alongside coyotes, wolves and dogs for thousands of years. Many of their legends tell of the close bond between animal and man. In one story, Coyote hears people worrying about the cold winter ahead. He runs into the mountains and steals fire from the beings that live there. Coyote brings fire back to the people, and teaches them how to make more fire by rubbing sticks together.

POOCH PARTNERS

Who are the owners of these famous dogs?

1. **Scooby Doo**
2. **Fluffy**
3. **Snowy**
4. **Santa's Little Helper**

Answers: 1. Shaggy 2. Hagrid (from the Harry Potter stories) 3. Tintin 4. Bart Simpson

CANINE CHARACTERS

96 **Greyfriars Bobby stayed by the grave of his owner for 14 years.** Bobby was a Skye terrier and was so devoted to his master, John Gray, that when he died in 1858, Bobby followed the coffin to the Greyfriars graveyard and stood guard, leaving only to get food, until his own death many years later.

▲ It has been reported that many people used to gather near the graveyard at one o'clock just to see Bobby leaving for his midday meal.

97 **Wallace and Gromit are a fine example of one man's friendship with his dog.** Wallace may be the human in the relationship, but the brains belong to his patient pooch, Gromit. These wonderful animated characters have appeared in several award-winning films, including *The Wrong Trousers*, *A Close Shave* and *The Curse of the Were-Rabbit*.

▶ Wallace, a cheese-loving inventor, and his faithful dog Gromit were created by animator Nick Park and first appeared on film in 1989.

There are award ceremonies worldwide to honour brave and loyal dogs.

98

In the story *Peter Pan and Wendy*, the Darling children are looked after by a Newfoundland dog called Nana. When Mr Darling decides that Nana must not sleep in the children's nursery any more, Peter Pan visits the children and persuades them all to fly away with him to Neverland. Mr Darling is so sorry for his actions that he sleeps outside in Nana's kennel until the children's safe return.

I DON'T BELIEVE IT!

Basset hounds have difficulty swimming, so bassets on boats should always be given their own lifejackets!

▲ When Peter Pan took Wendy and the boys to Neverland, Mr Darling was left in the doghouse!

99

Snoopy is one of the world's most popular dog characters. This cartoon character is a beagle, who first appeared in a newspaper comic strip in the 1950s. Snoopy likes to lie on top of his doghouse, which is where he does most of his thinking. His owner is Charlie Brown, but Snoopy just sees him as the person who brings him his supper!

100

Endal, a yellow Labrador, was given the Dog of the Millennium Award in 1999. Endal got his special award for his service to his owner, who was a wheelchair-user. Endal could buy bus tickets and even use cash machines! Like many other pooches around the world Endal has proved that dogs are more than just pets – they are our friends, helpers and heroes!

INDEX

Page numbers in **bold** refer to main entries.